IN THE KINGDOM OF THE WILDERNESS

IN THE KINGDOM OF THE WILDERNESS

LARRY KIMPORT

In The Name Publishing

In The Name Publishing
PO Box 101
Perry, KS 66073

Ann Brooks - Cover Design
Kristen Robbs - Editing

First Printing, 2024

ISBN - 979-8-9876159-8-0

For Nina and Reuben,
and the house with the straw roof.

Thank you, Pastor Charles Heaps,
for being kind.

Road to Jericho

~ One ~

I was stirring our small fire when the sun rose beyond distant hills. We were packed and ready, for we feared being followed.

It was cold by this time of year—the month of December, the final month of the Roman calendar. We Jews knew it as the time when the rains came to Judea, but for the Romans, distant and near, it marked the celebration of their great holiday of Saturnalia, the closing of their year.

I myself was nearing my forty-seventh year with my third child at my bosom. A child born to me late in life, from the promises of a coppersmith who I never believed to begin with. It would seem loneliness makes us childlike. He'd been my master and had told me repeatedly that he appreciated my humble earnestness as I labored within his family's home. In the dark, he whispered that he liked my womanly curves. Beneath my wrappings, he imagined my aging rump and legs to be heavier and stronger, fleshy soldiers of my life's toil. Upon my child's birth, I was dismissed from service to be forgotten.

~ Two ~

There were twenty-four of us escaping Jerusalem, headed across the wilderness for Lydda by way of Emmaus, as decided by the men of the two families my daughter and I now served. Four nights before we had approached the caravan, desperate to escape the burnings. Unwanted as comrades, we offered ourselves as servants. The men had excused us briefly, arguing amongst themselves, before accepting our terms.

Thus, we joined them in service and in flight.

Journeying alone through the wilderness would have been too perilous with our little ones, not to mention our few sheep, our goat, and our two burros. I remember those burros well: one was naughty, the other nice. Both were burdened with all we owned.

The smoke from the burning of Jerusalem darkened the sky behind us as the men studied the rocky trail ahead, intending to alter our course hard west, but deciding to give up Lydda and aim for Jericho instead. The evening before, two of them had ventured farther ahead. When they returned, they announced distant smoke lying unnatural upon our northern horizon—likely more work of the Romans. But the men seemed to breathe easier, noting our aloneness as far as they could see. I stole snippets of their discussion, straining to hear them over the cold wind that flapped at our outer wraps.

Kneeling by our small fire, I opened my underrobe and kissed my infant child. This baby, my third, was my second born out of wedlock. Only my first child, now lost to me, had been born to me proper, in a good home, long ago at the end of my own childhood.

Then there was my second-born, my limping Elizabeth, twenty years old and kneeling beside me at that same small fire. Both Elizabeth and this infant were children of wrongs from a life I am not proud of.

Elizabeth was speaking to her son, Samuel, comforting him as he shivered from the cold. The sight prodded a deep ache within me; I had lost my own firstborn some thirty years before. Not to death, but to my husband when he expelled me from his family's home. In doing so, he kept our son. I have watched for them in my wanderings forever after.

The sun broke through as we moved out, our fire put out behind us. We journeyed onward, laboring into the rising of the Judean hills before us, our animals a bleating and braying mass.

We warmed from walking as our path grew softer beneath the sparse cypresses and cedars. Our animals crowded us through the trees, but we could still hear the men conversing, reminiscing about when Rome herself had burned six years prior. It was known that the great city had burned wildly and thoroughly, and the citizens of her empire were restless without a target to blame. We in Judea cared little, learning of the burning months after it happened, but the topic still foddered many a conversation.

"Rumor has it," one called to another, "that Emperor Nero, fancying himself a great poet and musician, was behind it himself, a great drama before a great backdrop."

The other man, his brother, switched at two goats, then answered, "Most figure the fire to be an accident. Of course, some blame the Superstitious."

I listened hard while leading my burro, for this was risky talk, this talk of the Superstitious, especially as the two families we served did not know each other well.

"Those heretics," the brother continued, "have wandered far in their evil secrecy—originating, some say, from our own beloved Judea."

His words would return to haunt us as our caravan journeyed onward beneath those trees. He did not know, nor did I, that one of *them* was amongst us that very morning.

For they, the Superstitious, are who and what my tale is about.

~ Three ~

Those were the hardest of times, when we of Judea clung to the written memories and wisdom of our Talmud and the directives of our lawgivers. Those were days of seeking solace from the proclamations of our Zealots and Pharisees, from cherished tales of great days long past, recalling our collective history of struggles, truths, and beauties— we, the chosen People of Abraham, clinging to our three thousand years of bondage, triumphs, and sorrows.

Four years before that morning upon that trail, our people had risen in righteous rebellion. Briefly, we breathed free behind the swords of our Zealots as Nero killed himself in far-off Rome, fenced in by his own flaws. The Emperor's death meant little to us in our own sad struggle of toil and bondage, an echo of our ancestors' building of great pyramids in times and lands distant and for a people more foreign than these present Romans. Our suffering seemed only repeated now in these hard times upon our own edge of Rome's great empire, obeying a great city we twenty-four would never see.

Only a single season before that morning, a man called

Vespasian had sent his son Titus to forcefully reclaim Jerusalem.

And Titus did come—burning, murdering, and scattering our people, a ruthless siege meant to break us forevermore as we refused to bow ourselves again to Rome's requisite devotion to her own gods, exacted by sword, bow, or spear-headed shaft.

~ Four ~

Before I tell more, my own name is Rebecca.

My family upon that trail consisted simply of myself, my newborn infant, my daughter Elizabeth, and her son Samuel.

Of the two families we served, the larger was comprised of twelve people: an elderly man and his two grown sons, all three weavers; the sons' wives, whom Elizabeth and I took our directives from; six children; and an aged woman who seldom spoke. The two adult brothers were proud Zealots of our faith and quite shrewd to be still amongst the living.

The other, smaller family consisted of three sisters and a man, evidently the husband of one of them—a gentle man, a potter and brick maker, often surrounded by his four children.

While moving amongst the beasts and the children that morning, I overheard a discourse within the larger family between the weavers and their wives, talk that grew urgent and tense. One of the wives suspected one of the three sisters to be a Follower of the Great Superstition.

Elizabeth and I listened in silence for the Great Superstition was something we knew all too well.

*

This harsh talk was sudden to Elizabeth and me. The last we knew, the men of both families had been conversing comfortably of a great island discovered beyond the shores of Gaul in the waters of the great Ocean Atlanticus, called Britannia by its own people and tamed for the Empire.

"In waters none know the end of!" claimed the potter.

But the weavers' words turned hard as we moved against the December wind, sharpened by their own women's suspicions. The gentle potter defended the accused woman. his wife or sister-in-law, Elizabeth and I could not tell.

My Elizabeth limped beside me. She had a failing within her right side, apparent since her first steps among my father's flocks, where I had returned upon my divorce.

"Are you following this talk, Mother?" she asked. "Do you hear this trouble stewing?"

"Hush! It is nothing to us." I freed my baby from my wraps and handed him to Elizabeth. Several days before I had lied to the families, leading them to believe my infant to be Elizabeth's while I passed myself off as a recent widow. My reasoning was simple: I did not wish to be thought of as an aging whore. My daughter's lone child, Samuel, was only four, and Elizabeth was still wet with milk, making my deception that much easier.

"But I pity her, Mother. She has done nothing to them, nor their wives or children," Elizabeth said as she propped herself, suckling my baby to her own bosom while walking.

"It is none of our affair," I whispered back. "We have our own worries now, and I need not remind you, my daughter, we harbor our own secrets as well. And aside from the infant, Elizabeth, *He* is your secret too—a shame we do not need. Not now. Not upon this trail fleeing Romans."

"But *we* are not of the Superstitious, Mother, so I do not fear," she replied as she petted the ears of our naughty burro laboring alongside us. My son was quiet at her breast, feeding.

Then came a fast bleating of the sheep. The goats hopped, spooked. The children of the families stiffened.

A caravan emerged upon the trail before us.

Fearful of the strangers, I spoke fast to Elizabeth. "Hush! The Zealots may hate the Romans, but they harbor no love for the Superstitious either. Remember that! For while there are no Romans upon this road"—I gripped her arm tightly and whispered harder—"the men may need something else to complain about. That is all. Our own secret has pained us enough; we do not need it upon this trail, amongst these people."

The unknown caravan materialized as four men and three boys leading a modest herd of tethered camels and asses.

Our two groups halted, and the men spoke and broke bread and shared water. The strangers were journeying westward, intending to deliver the animals to the men who'd bought them. They knew of the burning of

Jerusalem, but nothing of Romans nearby. We parted after pleasantries—us for Jericho, them for Lydda.

Silent and obedient, I looked over the men and the boys as carefully as I could, but I saw no familiarity in their features.

~ Five ~

Late in the morning we came upon a small stream. A stretch of cedar and oak hugged the brook as it tumbled westward, bound for the distant River Jordan.

The weaver's oxen pulled their three carts forward to the stream's edge; the potter's family followed with two of their own. All five were packed and tied high with all they could manage, and the bundles rocked and swayed with the oxen's exertions. The two families corralled their sheep, goats, and burros toward the fresh water. Strapped atop four burros contained within light pens were cocks and hens. The families also had three milking cows between them.

Elizabeth and I carefully led our two burros to the water. We drank heavily, beast and man alike, then filled our pots and sacks upstream from the animals that muddied the water, bleating and braying. Elizabeth and Samuel hurried with their work, then returned to me.

"They're still discussing it, Mother," Elizabeth told me, keeping her voice low, "that one woman's faith, or *Him*." Her hands, cold and wet, struggled to strap our water as she added, "or perhaps both of them."

I advised her sharply: "You may listen, but add nothing."

The women of the families were quiet, resting, as the men resumed their conversation.

"...based on the wanderings of a criminal, a heretic who died forty years ago," stated the old man.

Elizabeth, stacking yet more water sacks, moved slowly by the stream, listening—for this criminal was our own great secret.

"Was He from Nazareth or Capernaum?" the younger son asked.

"He was a carpenter, or at least His father was," his brother answered confidently.

"Both worked wood," conceded their father. Concerning the heretic's home, however, he was not so certain, for lies and tales were common, taking on lives of their own.

*

Of course, beneath those cedars and oaks my secret burned within me: the man from forty years prior, our peoples' great heretic, was my own mother's brother.

He was of my very own family.

Our secret and our pride, our fear and our truth.

A ghost, sailing through the winds of our times.

~ Six ~

My mother's mother, my grandmother, was called Mary.

Across her years she gave birth to three daughters, the second being my own mother.

These daughters were born interspersed amongst her sons: James, Joses, Simon, and Jude. All were born to her and to my grandfather, Joseph, after their firstborn came to them in Mary's fifteenth year.

The heretic who spawned such spreading tales, the very one the men debated beside that small stream, was that firstborn child, born nearly seventy years prior.

My mother's oldest brother, the one named *Jesus*.

~ Seven ~

I helped Elizabeth strap the last of our water upon our burros—a task worthy of two, as the naughty one bucked.

"Did you hear anything else?" I whispered to her. "Of the Superstitious?"

Elizabeth looked cold. She shivered as she answered, almost too loudly, "Only the tales we've already heard—silly notions of magic and sayings and such." She wouldn't meet my eyes.

"My aunts, Elizabeth, believe much of His wanderings and doings. So do two of my uncles—His own brothers. But my mother did not, nor do I, I must remind you."

"There was something of His being born a Roman edict," Elizabeth interrupted me. "Perhaps for a census. The weavers disagreed about where this happened, if at all. One claimed Capernaum. The old man cited Samaria." She paused as she tightened her ropes, fastening her water while rocking our headstrong burro, before adding, "the quieter man claimed Bethlehem, or so he had heard."

I felt old as I shifted my infant beneath my robe. I had taken him back; he was content, his belly full of my and Elizabeth's milk.

As Elizabeth tethered our burros, I remembered how shameful I had been to my own parents. Then, as the men moved us out, I thought instead of His shames, brought upon my family when I was still a little girl. Shames that seemed to be growing in the strangest of ways so long after His death.

Distant, low howls came from the hills to the north, breaking my sad thoughts.

Wolves.

Our animals shivered and quieted. The men spread out.

Gripping the reins of our naughty burro, I returned to my thoughts, pondering how so much would have been so different if He had just stayed with His carpenter work, shaping useful things from Judea's cypress and oak.

Or fishing, or shepherding. Anything other than His drawing of the crowds, beckoning to those who followed Him.

~ Eight ~

By early afternoon we had trekked into higher, rockier ground, and by mid-afternoon we rested amongst large rocks atop a wind-swept crest.

The men chose this spot for its farseeing advantage, though they remained pleased to be so alone in that wilderness. The wolves had dropped off, and the horizon about us was free of unwanted smoke and dust. Only the wind seemed to be with us, pushing at us as we refreshed ourselves from our stores of water.

Elizabeth and I settled between large stones toward the rear of our movement. Samuel, after drinking heartily, ventured forward towards the other children.

"You've been quiet, Mother. Are you alright?" Elizabeth asked.

"Yes, I'm fine. I am just tired."

"Are you certain? Let me carry the baby." She held her arms out.

"That would nice, just for a bit. Thank you." I passed him over then lay my head back.

"You are welcome. Perhaps he'll feed."

Elizabeth opened her tunic for my child, then

murmured, "Tell me about Him, Mother. Please. The others are resting ahead, beyond hearing."

"Tell you of whom?" I was tired and couldn't imagine who she was asking about. The cooling breeze sounded through the large rocks.

"Of *Him*, Mother— your mother's eldest brother. I haven't asked in so long, since before John's death. You never speak of Him, and—"

"And I'll not speak of Him now, Elizabeth," I cut her off. "As though we have no problems of our own, amongst these families we travel with!" Then I paused. "Have you been thinking of your husband? Of John?"

"No, not too much. I only ask due to the suspicions concerning the youngest of the three sisters."

"Now is not the time; no time shall be. I know nearly nothing. Who does? He was killed long ago," I whispered, unnecessarily.

The breeze continued to whip fast through the large rocks. Sheep bleated amongst lowing cows around our resting. I looked toward the noise, thinking how very little I had shared with Elizabeth over the years of what I'd heard, and come to be ashamed of regarding Him.

"You know everything that I know," I assured her, tamping my conscience, "and most of it is lies and silly superstitions. You've never been foolish, Elizabeth. Keep to the truths of our faith. Pay no mind to stories of magic and queer things said. His fights with the scribes and the rabbis were shameful, if even partly true, and more shameful if made up!"

Elizabeth still sitting beside me said nothing, so I went

on. "And it is made up, all of it! Look at the state of things. Look at us and these two families crossing this wilderness —fleeing. Look at our people—murdered and burned out. All has come undone, my child. Not *saved*!" By the end, my voice had risen, begging her to understand.

No one looked back from the two families resting ahead of us. The children played atop large rocks. Neither Elizabeth nor I trusted little Samuel at such frolic, so we kept our eyes on him as I finished quieter, "I do not like being sharp with you, my daughter, and certainly not with my own son at your bosom. Speak no more of this. Of Him."

Then I stood, working at our gentler burro's packs, unfastening bread and a handful of almonds to complement our water. The clouds above moved with the wind across the sky: cool, promising more December rains to come. I looked up into the grayness.

I had not been fully truthful, for I had not only heard the tales and accusations concerning my mother's eldest brother, I had witnessed a few firsthand. As a little girl I had met Him on two separate occasions.

But I stayed quiet beneath that moving sky, sorting my almonds and bread amongst those large rocks on that path to Jericho.

~ Nine ~

I was seven years old when I first met Him.

It was within a small, mud-bricked home; whose, I don't know. I can remember a cat and the play of children about and, of course, Him—my mother's brother, standing in the middle of the room, moving towards the door-way. Perhaps He was leaving; I think someone was angry with Him.

But as I sat upon that wind-swept crest all those years later, my thoughts turned to the other time I met Him. I remember it more clearly, so I've kept it more secret.

I was nine or ten, and I was sitting upon His lap. There were others about. We were gathered beneath a grove of trees—fruit of one sort or another. I recall looking into His eyes and tasting His very breath, for He spoke directly to me.

His words were deliberate for my being such a little girl. My shepherding family, traveling between Capernaum and Magdala, had come upon Him on the western banks of our inland Sea of Galilee.

He was situated amongst a crowd composed of those

who followed Him everywhere. Some loved Him, I suppose; the others were simply curious.

Resting in the grove He was soft-spoken and kind, asking me about my mother, my family and our flocks. He listened intently, and He told me that I and my family, like everyone, was cared for in a very special way by our loving God.

~ Ten ~

Of course, I said nothing to my daughter as I thought of my mother's family of carpenters and my father's family of shepherds. Then my thoughts wandered to Jared, my childhood friend—ghostly images of gentleness and hope. Days and nights returned to me, some especially sunny, others starry or moony.

I shook my head and returned instead to the shade of that grove again, sitting upon His gentle lap and asking why so many disliked Him. He seemed so kind, yet the words spoken of Him were often harsh and fearful.

He smiled, then told me a story. I remember His hair and His eyes as I sat with Him, and that our families' sheep were in the tale. One was lost, which had to be found.

Then I asked if I would see Him again, for He wandered about so much.

He answered, "Seek yourself, little Rebecca, in the reflection of the pooled stream. Observe the pureness of the child you see looking back at you, for then you'll see innocence and faith, the blessings of children. Then think of Me."

I did not understand. I pressed my matter. "But will I talk to You again? I fear the anger so many have for you."

I recalled, amongst those wind-swept rocks, that He was smaller than most men, yet moved as though large. About Him, others moved carefully and thoughtfully.

"You can speak to Me anytime," He had told me. "I'll hear you, and I will listen."

Then He talked to me about tenderness. I remember the cool high grass and the sunny sky above as He gently rocked me, urging me not to fear for Him but to hold and keep love and faith and allow them into my heart.

Beneath those citrus trees, He had told me, "Faith and prayer and gentle behavior all serve one another. This comes more easily to children. Grown-ups would do well to study them."

~ Eleven ~

Sitting amongst those rocks, weary and pained of quarreling, I wondered of my mother's brother's faith and prayer. Moreover, I wondered if He had erred. I did not understand His promises, for in due time His own end came upon a Roman cross of wood and nails.

And He did perish upon that cross, for my parents and the rabbis and the lawgivers all said so, despite the rumors spread by the Superstitious. Hence, I kept the memories of His words within myself.

I spread our almonds upon a flat rock, setting aside a small pile for Samuel upon his return from the other children. While doing so, I tried to recall if my mother's brother had spoken to me before or after His *Hard Saying*, as some later called it. Others called it His *Sermon On The Mount*. Either way, they meant a divisive speech by Him that rent the crowds who followed Him into true believers and those, befuddled and angered, who lost faith.

They say, during this teaching, that He called Himself the "Bread of Life" and claimed that God was no more in our temple than anywhere else, for He is everywhere. And, like the Romans or worse- for distant Rome at least allowed us some of our laws—He claimed that our most sacred law, the beloved law handed down from Abraham through Moses and beyond, that by which we live, must now defer to some law of His. A single law, deep within each of us, as though we are somehow worthy of such a thing. A single law, greater than the collection of those within our beloved Talmud.

Squinting into the bracing wind, I recalled a time in His wandering when many lost hope in Him, calculating the years that weaved His ministry and the end of His life against my own childhood, comparing the times when I heard talk of Him, almost always bad, against the present tales shared about Him.

As I added sprinkles of prunes and bread from my haversack atop Samuel's almonds, I recalled more of His words to me, spoken as I sat upon His lap beneath those trees.

He had told me, "Faith and prayer and good works are all one and the same, little Rebecca. This is easy for children, for they are more trusting. It was much harder for a Roman soldier I met, who came to me in a village once."

"How so?" I braved to ask.

"This Roman had to cast his faith strong for a servant girl, a girl who meant little to him, but was loved dearly by someone close to him. He came to Me, asking Me to save this servant, all for someone else's love. And this is important, for loving others is always important. So, it will come to you too, little one. Listen to your faith. Listen to it for Me, and a great peace shall await you."

"I miss my friend, Jared," I dared further. "Shall I pray for him?"

"Yes, you should. He is lonely, and he longs for you. He has whispered his own faith into the wind."

*

Later, while sitting beside a small fire with my beloved Jared, I had nearly told him of this event. Our families' sheep had been quiet as my shepherd boy told me that he loved me, that he wished to marry me one day, to unite our flocks, and to care for me.

Now, upon that damp wilderness trail, I thought of his little boy wishes as I rose from the rocks; the men had called us into moving.

Samuel returned. Elizabeth cleaned his hands and arms up to his elbows, as our law prescribed, so he could eat while walking.

Just over the rocky crest, distant gazelles bounded away from fears unseen by us. The wind blew hard, pushing the gray away. The Khamsin, we called those winds—winds from the lands of Babylon.

~ Twelve ~

By sunset we came upon a shallow ravine.

After some discussion, the men had us prod our loaded animals down into the dry creek bed to pitch our coverings for the night. Despite the recent light rains, there was no stream, so we had to be prudent with our water. We were fortunate for wood, however, for we happened upon two fallen oaks downed from past rushing waters.

We ate, warmed by the fire, as quiet talk between the families turned to the lost Temple of Mount Moriah. Built a thousand years before, it had enshrined the Ark of the Covenant, but it had since been defiled, destroyed, and rebuilt, time and time again, as first Persia, then Egypt, Babylon, and Syria all took their turns wresting Jerusalem from our forefathers.

"And so it is in our own time," the elder weaver spoke. "Herod's Temple has been destroyed as Rome takes her own turn at our people's home on Earth."

"Only a single wall remains," his brother lamented.

The fire flickered as the smaller children poked at the coals beneath while the older ones listened intently to the men's conversation, their wide eyes reflecting the licking of the fire's flames.

The men turned to more contemporary talk, discussing a certain Saul of Tarsus.

"Once a seeker and a great defamer of the Superstitious, then he became one of them!" the elder weaver spat.

"Now he goes by Paul," the weaver's father added, "and he's spreading this madness north, even into Syria."

~ Thirteen ~

Elizabeth, with little Samuel lying beside her, listened intently as did I within the small cover of our leaning shelter. For we knew this talk would lead to my mother's brother; it always did. The name Saul also stirred me.

As I cradled my baby, warm within my wraps, my thoughts returned to my own firstborn, my Saul. His young face flashed before me, as though within a strong dream, and jolted me awake by the side of the fire. Then, as I watched sparks swirl up into the darkness, I thought again of Jared. My mind and heart were torn between the two losses of my life, haunted first by memories of my son's face, followed by Jared and myself as children tending sheep along the grassy banks of the River Hasbani. I recalled a warm night when Jared and I shared ourselves in a most tender way, without elders or brothers or sisters about. We had observed our sheep and our dogs couple often enough across our shepherding youths, and we quietly talked of what that singular duty would be like for ourselves, wondering of its beauty.

Beneath the moonlight that streaked down through the coconut palms, we quietly inspected one another through partial disrobing, without touching each other—preparing ourselves for after we married.

Both of us, as children, were pleased that night beneath the thousand stars.

*

Shortly after, I was promised to the son of a money-changer from Bethsaida, from the northeastern shore of the Sea of Galilee. He was of a fine family, my father informed me. My mother reminded me not to shame our own.

My husband's name was Amon. Nearing thirty years himself, he was far into his adulthood, and his parents were earnest to find him a bride. I myself was but thirteen.

~ Fourteen ~

Amon was a good fortune for me, or so my mother told me. She insisted that my marriage to him was a blessing, given the shame we carried over her eldest brother.

Then sad memories whirled their way through my mind: applying ointments to Amon's skin; our hushed labor of man and woman within the darkness of his father's home, our companionship wanting; my laying beneath Amon, thin planks away from the bed of his two fat sisters, my sisters now, to whom I must be good and kind in this, their home. All the duties of married life, alongside the daily grindings of wheat and barley for our bread, the collecting of wild honey, the drying of dates and figs, and the hauling of fresh water from the local well.

Oh how I missed my family and my curly-haired shepherd boy, all westward across the River Hasbani! A lifetime away for a young shepherd girl.

A crackling of sparks exploded from within the fire, the light bouncing across the sides of the ravine. The embers climbed up into the night, sweeping me back into the present, away from my childhood of starry nights and gentle hills. I marked my marriage as the ending of my childhood in every way, except the one I secretly treasured; for while making a home with Amon and his sisters and parents, while laying for Amon at his pleasure, I still longed for my Jared, still amongst the sheep and the streams of the north country.

I attempted to send word to him, first through a servant girl I knew from the wells— a girl run off from Bethsaida for stealing from her employer—to no avail.

Then I tried again, through the attentiveness of a passing-through Roman soldier. For some reason he listened; perhaps he was homesick himself.

My messages were brief. They read, as I entrusted the soldier,

> *Greetings.*
> *I miss you. I yet cling to our intentions.*
> *Do not forget me.*

I desperately wished that I could read and write, for the strength of those careful markings I saw at the Temple and among Amon's and his father's figures seemed so worthy of my own heart's sorrow. But no matter, my Jared was without that skill as well.

I never received a response from him, in note or otherwise.

Then, hard words erupted within the ravine, disrupting my recollections. A new discussion was hard upon the two families, as fractious as the sparks leaping from the flames of the fire.

~ Fifteen ~

Popping sparks swirled skyward as the elder weaver proclaimed, "We have suspicions you know!"

The potter rose from tending the fire and challenged him, "I do not listen to you, man."

Elizabeth whispered to me, "I have figured it out—he is married to the stumpy one, the middle one."

"Elizabeth, please, keep a mind to our—"

"Mother, the weavers believe one of the three sisters to be a Follower. I plan to watch closely for which it is, and I would guess not the potter's stumpy wife."

"Do not listen to me then!" the old man spoke loudly. "Listen to the simplest of reasons that even the Romans understand. It's altogether abhorrent, the claim of these fanatics, believing that a criminal's corpse crawled forth from its own grave to become a 'King of Kings!'"

"And you may add to that, my father," spoke the younger weaver, the fire reflected in his eyes, "that few people knew of Him when He was roaming about. And I have heard, from reputable men, that those who did happen upon Him and cared to listen, cared even less afterward."

Then, content with having put the potter and his family in their place, their tones softened, and talk shifted to other topics. The women shuffled about preparing the children for bed, the older ones protesting as the younger ones began bedding beneath the shelters.

Elizabeth and I watched from within our own small shelter, little Samuel between us, happy for the brief peace that would not last. For once the children were asleep, we were taken again by sudden talk of my mother's brother.

The men would not leave Him be.

*

Listening to the men debate cautiously about the fire and quieting my baby who had begun to cry, I recalled further details from my first encounter with Him in that house long ago. There had been talk in that house of another man, a prisoner who had loved and believed in my mother's brother. I shuddered, recalling that for his love for Him, that man's head had been cut off as a favor for some woman. *John*—that was the name whispered in my long-buried memory.

The brothers talked on across the fire, but I did not listen, turning instead to Elizabeth. "Shall we sleep?"

"Yes, Mother. I've spread our blankets." She lowered her voice. "I hope they cease."

"They will. It is late, and we have other concerns to worry over."

"Yes, like water. We'll have to find some early to fill up all around. We are all running low."

*

Then another story revisited me as I covered us with our

blankets. It was from the second time I saw my mother's brother, when He spoke to me in the shade of that citrus grove. He had been making His way south for Jerusalem. Such a gentle man, and yet so, so wrong. Even then there were whispers of what awaited Him there: hatred and fear armed with thick timbers and heavy nails. I do not remember from whom I first heard that talk. But I do know they were grownups, and they were men, and they told such scary stories for a little girl to overhear when her shepherding parents did not know she was listening.

Inside our small shelter, I tried hard to think of other things, listening to the fire as my baby sighed deep in sleep. Elizabeth and Samuel were also still. I heard only their breathing accompanied by pops and sizzles from the fire. Then the startling thrush of added wood—someone was up, tending the fire.

Little Samuel stirred beside me. I settled him, then lay quiet, attentive to the distant clamor of hyenas we must have disturbed.

There were voices too—the three weavers, quietly determining to rid themselves of the Follower of the Superstition.

Night of Thieves

~ Sixteen ~

After leaving the ravine, we came at last upon a brook where we replenished our sacks and jugs. Distant tendrils of our fire bent in the sky behind us, pushed by the scattered white clouds that moved from the east.

Not far from the brook, the two brothers climbed high rocks and reported seeing distant men on horseback. There were two of them, little more than dark flickers atop the next rise. The weavers guessed the horsemen to be lone travelers, perhaps pausing to wonder over our own dark trailing figures across the same distance.

Or maybe Romans—a thought we feared to speak. Perhaps sentries, forward scouts for a larger number, perhaps a legion stationed nearby. The four weavers talked amongst themselves of this possible Roman cavalry who must be mounted and mobile, seeing to their ordered "Great Scattering" of us Jews, dutiful in their role to keep things moving along.

Then the men pondered instead the rocky highlands we were descending. The old man seemed to know the most.

"They run north and south. They're called the 'Samarian

Hills' east of Galilee," he claimed, "and just 'The Hills' farther south. A long, gentle spine in the land."

He gazed across the expanse. "Just two days more to Jericho," he reckoned as we readied ourselves to move on ever farther from the burned-out Jerusalem we sorely missed. I listened in as the three sisters spoke lovingly and longingly of their former homes: strong homes, unlike those of us shepherding people. Homes walled with thick brick, making cool, dark rooms partitioned by wood.

Homes like that of Amon's family.

I had given birth within such a house, upon Amon's bed of straw and wool. A home governed by Amon's father, shared with his ugly sisters. A place where I learned to lay quietly beneath my husband, learning his skin and his smell. A home and a grave, the death site of my childhood where I went about my duties as Amon's wife while Amon went about his. A burdensome place, learning his father's business of trading and markets near and far, yoked to the cruelty of Roman taxes. A sad place, haunted still by a ghostly dance of images all these years later after fleeing that life, greatly shaming my husband and his family.

For I slipped away from them all, fleeing into the north country with my infant in my arms, into the hills of the shepherds, seeking the grassy banks of the River Hasbani in search of my Jared.

I couldn't stay in Amon's family home any longer, not after a neighbor's servant passed on a story told by traveling magicians of a dying boy who sought his lost love. This dying youth was a shepherd boy, passing slowly to the wrenching of the yellow vomit, all the while calling for his lost shepherd girl, married off to a rich man's un-deserving son.

I'd vanished in the middle of a night, taking half the denarii I had brought into my marriage. I'd run for three full moons, my suckling firstborn at my young bosom, begging and lying and story-telling my way across the land, desperate to return to my first love.

But I failed, and upon my return, my husband properly divorced me.

~ Seventeen ~

The men, watching the horizon, moved us further through the hills, meandering our line down into stronger grasses.

Elizabeth and I brought up the rear of our movement until the weavers stopped our party abruptly and called me forward. They called the potter forward as well.

With my baby wrapped tightly to my bosom, I cautiously led our better-behaved burro to the weavers and offered them water. The men took it silently, busy gazing upon the remains of a gazelle.

The animal, cast off the stony trail, had been cut in half—less than a day before, the men figured. Its back half was missing, cut neatly away, while the charred remains of a fire smoldered between two nearby large rocks. The two sons guessed the animal to be the handiwork of the scouts spotted earlier. The potter, however, disagreed.

Kneeling in the morning breeze, he spoke quietly, "The Romans take much from the land, as they take from everywhere, but they travel hard, with purpose, and would never abandon even half a gazelle."

The old weaver, looking tired, stayed silent. He too

knew that the Romans took great stock of their stores as they moved. However, he said nothing until the potter returned to his family. Then he quietly told his sons, "We must watch the horizons for the lone riders, whoever they may be."

We left the carcass of the gazelle and moved on eastward, watchful as we made our way out of those Samarian Hills.

*

The breeze eased, and the sun poured its warmth down upon our backs before we stopped again, choosing to rest upon a grassy expanse of level ground, descending the highlands. A flexing cloud of small birds moved in the distance, southbound.

It was a good place for feeding the children the men figured, and fine ground for the animals to graze. Visibility was suitable, for we had seen the distant riders again, ahead of us but closer now. Moreover, another group had been spotted to the south of our movement by the three sisters: three or four horsemen moving parallel to us amongst far rocks and scattered trees.

The men agreed that neither group behaved like Romans of any sort and this was frightening, for their movements seemed cautious and calculated, as though stalking us beneath the December sun still high in the sky.

Aware of these fellow travelers, we took time to settle ourselves, all the while hoping for friendlier companions to appear. Traders, fellow scattered brethren—anyone at all would do. The women arranged salted mutton and bread with shaking hands, accompanied with water, prunes, and some of the poorer wine. Elizabeth and I, fearful as well, asked the women of both families if we could lead the communal washing to the elbows and subsequent prayers.

~ Eighteen ~

We ate upon our blankets, watchful for any movement distant or near. Even the suspicion regarding the faith of the youngest of the three sisters had died down, though it hadn't disappeared. Uneasy whispers made their way through the camp. She and the Great Superstition were too easy to blame for any misfortune to come.

Elizabeth sensed this and mentioned it to me. I hushed her. "They've shared their meat and their bread with us, to add to the last of our poor wine and nuts. Be thankful."

"But, Mother, even if we are being followed, it is not and cannot be that woman's doing."

"I know too much about finding fault; I wish no part of it," I whispered. "Condemning or defending it."

This much was true, particularly given who my uncle was and all the sorrow and confusion He'd provoked during His own time and beyond. I had further had this lesson etched on my heart following my divorce at sixteen, when Amon had expelled me from his father's home as the scribes and Chief Priest saw fitting.

My bosom still wet with milk, I had begged Amon to not

send me off. I'd pleaded from my knees before his door, before his family, not to separate me from my infant.

But one of Amon's sisters had fallen gravely ill, and his mother blamed this misfortune on me, her son's harlot bride, his wife from a suspect, shepherding family. The accusation wrested away mercy. The door shut firmly to me.

Eating with the others upon that trail, I knew unfounded blame all too well.

"It just isn't fair, Mother."

"I know, Elizabeth. I truly do. Now, get enough to eat and see that little Samuel does too."

"Do you think that she is...well...among the Superstitious?"

"I do not know, nor do I care. Please, Elizabeth, leave it be."

And I didn't care. I truly didn't, having long ago surrendered to my life of service amongst those who begged most humbly for work, security, and companionship. A life amongst those justly stoned or left to die, struck fast to wood if caught sinning or wronging those above us.

Crucifixion. A death I knew too well. One reserved for the most lowly of criminals.

In little time we finished our feeding and repacked the backs of our beasts.

By late afternoon we came upon another stream, one swollen with the recent rains. It tumbled and pooled cold beneath scattered poplars and cedars amongst large rocks.

With the sun low in the sky, the men decided that we would stay there for the night. The strangers, both sets, were glimpsed again before us and beside us. Those beside us were the same who'd appeared south of us earlier in the day. Elizabeth and I saw them and reported our sightings to the men. We discerned four on horseback, gaining on us in a flickering, slow way, as though they were waiting on the setting sun.

"We will build a single fire of thinner wood," the elder weaver instructed.

We huddled together about its warmth between our pitched shelters. In unspoken fear we ate and rested, the sun setting beyond the highlands we'd crossed.

*

The night was moonless and cold. Just beyond the dancing reaches of our small fire, the animals settled beneath the cedars and poplars.

Then they suddenly stirred in the near darkness, braying and lowing, giving way to the dark figures of four horsemen.

The older brother spoke first, "Who comes to us? Answer me so that I may welcome you to our fire."

"Travelers," their own leader spoke, his voice soft but raspy. "On our way eastward," he added, which gave us hope of their passing through.

Then the rest of the strangers appeared one at a time, stepping into our firelight: three men on horses, and a boy on a burro. The boy was dark-skinned with big eyes.

"How may we be of kindness?" the weaver spoke again.

The potter came to his side followed by the other brother. The children were silent and still amongst the women as we watched from within our shelters.

"We shall see," their leader answered. "We have stores of food that we can share."

"I see, and I thank you," spoke the elder brother. "We too can share from our stores for your company." His brother and the potter nodded in agreement.

The three men dismounted while the boy stayed on his burro. Two of the strangers' feet were wrapped in rags; both were younger men.

The strangers acknowledged the weavers' aged father who had emerged slowly from the larger shelter. Two of the strangers spoke quietly in Syrian accents with the weavers about the weather, their spotting us as we had seen them, and their day of traveling. They knew of the burning of Jerusalem, but nothing of Romans about.

The old man, his fear somewhat abated, confirmed all of us to be Jews, strangers and families alike, and in a mutual covenant with God, desiring to bring our fireside encounter to an unspoken peace. His younger son mentioned the killing of a hen and libating of some proper wine.

Then splashes came from the stream behind us. Our sheep bleated as two more horsemen appeared from the darkness: an older man followed by a woman. Her hair was ragged, and she was stout and dark-eyed like the boy who remained on his burro. We learned later that both were slaves.

By the small fire's light, it became clear that the six strangers knew one another. All turned quiet as the visitors spread themselves around us.

With no further command, they drew their glistening swords.

~ Nineteen ~

The small fire tumbled in on itself, flickering a strange light for the work of the thieves.

The younger weaver spoke first, "No one move!"

"No, man, you be still," the leader of the thieves spoke sharply. "Be still, and no one need die." Then he laughed, "Saturnalia Greetings! Behave and all shall be safe. On your knees now, you four," he commanded the weavers and the potter. "Hands behind your backs!"

Huddled within our shelters, we watched the men bow before the thieves' shimmering swords.

"Take the Follower instead!" a woman cried out from the largest tarp.

Then another voice, from within the same darkness, "She has brought your kind amongst us, she of the Great Superstition. You robbers are her madness—that same madness of the carpenter's son!"

The potter's children cried out as one figure rose gracefully, emerging from their shelter.

"Forgive these trespassers!" the youngest of the sisters called out. "Forgive these highway men for what they are going to do to us!"

"Anna, no!" cried the potter from his knees.

"Be still, you!" their leader commanded. "Do you not listen?"

Still the potter arched up, trying to stand, his arms behind himself.

"No, Anna!" he cried out again.

The leader drew his sword high and, in a single, two-handed motion, slashed the potter where his neck met his shoulders.

By the light of the fire, we watched the potter's upper body separate, splitting like fleshy wood as he pitched forward. Muffled screams cried out from within both coverings of tarp and again as the thief worked at freeing his sword.

"Silence!" their leader shouted, spinning about before casting fast orders to his fellow bandits.

The weavers stayed on their knees. The old man prayed, illuminated by the rhythm of flame, as one woman from within each of our coverings was dragged forth by the younger thieves. I cried softly within our own darkness as Elizabeth was pulled from me and Samuel, limping away, joining the others.

The thieves pushed the three women to the ground beside the kneeling men. Whips were drawn, demanding obedience. Then came more commands and the dismounting of the stout woman from her horse and the big-eyed boy from his burro.

All grew strangely quiet, save the stifled cries of the children. The potter remained face down, his blood pooling black beneath the licking flames of the fire.

The thieves argued fast amongst themselves. The aged weaver prayed aloud only to be whipped into silence. A separate command saw the stout woman move briskly, without expression, to pull a little girl from the shelter of the weavers. The child kicked and cried as she was dragged across the stones. Silently, the woman forced the girl down upon the rocky ground.

"Let this teach you all!" their leader spoke loudly as he drew a long knife from an unseen sheath. "Let this be your lesson. Do not disobey."

He then forcibly turned the girl's head as she flexed beneath the slave woman. The firelight flickered across her dark eyes as he pulled back her hair, grasped her ear, and sliced it free from her head.

Her cries were quick and high. More cries joined hers as the criminal tossed the severed ear into the fire. The stout woman steered the girl back to her family, and she vanished again into their darkness, her ear sizzling and smoking upon the coals as the raiders' work began in earnest.

*

With sword still drawn, the leader ordered one of the younger thieves to stay with the stout woman by their prisoners before the fire as the other thieves and the big-eyed boy worked through our stores and packings, one at a time.

After quarreling twice amongst themselves, they filled three sacks with bread, wild honey, heavy Roman denarii, jewelry, several fine blankets, and all the wine they could manage. They barked at the big-eyed boy to carry away their findings, then they returned to the men upon their knees.

Their leader spoke loudly to the weavers' father, "Who among you follows the Superstition?"

Silence followed, save the sounds of a crying child.

"Come now," he demanded, kicking the aged man backwards. "My cousin and I would like to see one of these Followers. It is said they slay their own children for their God—One believed to have crawled forth from His own grave. Dead, then risen!" He laughed at the last.

The fire popped and sizzled.

"Turka, fetch wood! We may stay a while longer."

The big-eyed boy scurried. The sheep bleated, and a cow lowed in the near dark.

"I ask again. Who amongst you is the Follower?"

The younger weaver answered hurriedly from his knees. "The youngest of the three sisters. She is in her family's shelter to your left."

"Yes, it is she!" A woman sobbed from within the weavers' covering. "It is she who has brought you amongst us!"

Their leader looked toward his helpers, who smiled. One though, the younger thief who had guarded us, looked frightened.

"Show yourself, woman! Bless us to see someone who embraces this madness spreading amongst the poorest of the poor."

Within the potter's shelter there was rustling amongst their weeping children. Then, a sudden sobbing as the fire-lit figure of the youngest sister emerged once again.

"The carpenter from Nazareth has my faith," she spoke

softly. She stepped forward, thin in her wraps and heavily scarred from childhood pox. She too was crying, but still she raised her pocked face. "And I have His love this night."

The leader laughed. "As though being crazy and of such poor luck for your companions isn't enough, you are ugly too!"

The young girl hung her head, her face lost within her dangling hair.

"And our misfortune as well," another thief joined. "Your ugliness, that is. For we have grown weary of Aminah."

Three of the thieves laughed. The big-eyed boy tended the fire while the slave woman stood as still as the trees.

"Aminah serves us well," the leader continued, "but she smells like her horse. She is nice and fat, but she is also old and dry. So, entertain us, ugly girl. Why do you believe what you believe? Why does your family keep you after you turned on their faith? And tell us too," he smirked, "where is your carpenter God this night?"

"I do not know. Perhaps the answers to your questions are not for me to know."

Then a rustling near the fire drew their attention away.

~ Twenty ~

"Elizabeth!" I cried out. "*Elizabeth*!"

I panicked as my daughter rose to her feet before that fire.

The other young thief lashed at her.

"Leave her heart be!" my daughter trembled. "Take her in your way, or kill her, or rob her, but leave her faith be!"

"Be silent, Elizabeth!" I hissed.

"We have another one, do we? Another of the Superstitious?" asked their leader. "One who limps, I see. How is the rest of you?" he leered.

Then little Samuel dashed into the firelight to his mother's side.

"Come to me, woman. I will not harm the boy," the thief promised. "I have made my point. Perhaps *you* can tell me why you people believe what you believe."

Elizabeth hobbled closer, Samuel tucked beneath her arm. Her face flickered in the firelight.

"I do not know what I believe. I only wonder why it is that this carpenter's son—who did not say the things that the lawgivers wished Him to say, nor did the things that the Pharisees expected of Him—why it is that He cannot be our Promised One? I have wondered, do we, the people of Abraham, get to choose our Deliverer, or does Yahweh choose Him for us?"

"She says the sacred name!" shouted the aged weaver from his knees. "How can she? How can they? How can they dare to say His name? Heretics! They are the ruin of us!"

"Sinners!" shouted his son beside him. "Blasphemers!"

"Silence, you two!" commanded the bandit behind them, striking the younger weaver with the butt of his sword.

"Silence," repeated their leader, "or you will join your bold companion upon the stones."

Then he turned back to Elizabeth. "Perhaps we will choose you instead, to relieve Aminah for the Saturnalia." He laughed. "Perhaps she'll take the time to bathe."

Propped to her strong side, Elizabeth didn't move as the leader placed the tip of his sword to her face, holding her still as he reached into her tunic.

I placed my baby down upon our blankets, then scrambled forth into the fire's light.

"Samuel, into the tent," I ordered. Then I breathed heavily, "Choose me. Choose me for you and your men."

"Are you her sister or her mother?"

"Her sister," I lied, "and in better health. Choose me." I lowered my voice to a whisper. "Please, allow me to tell you why."

Intrigued, the leader moved his sword from Elizabeth's face to my own. He smirked, working its steel point into the corner of my mouth. "Do tell me why, woman. Do tell me why."

I kept my gaze fixed on his weathered eyes, my voice low. "She has the bugs. Once throughout the hair of her head, still throughout that...of her modesty. She's been ridden with the lice for half a year now."

Their leader turned his sword, cutting the inside of my mouth. His face flickered with the new light of the fire—the work of the big-eyed boy. "Why would you warn me? Why not allow her to infect us?"

"We may survive this night and happen upon one another again, where I'd fear your wrath."

"That is wise. But *you* are foolish, protecting a Follower."

"Choose me for you and your men," I repeated. "I can please you better than my sister."

"Then you shall," he grinned, digging his sword deeper with a twist.

Then he took me by my hair across the stream, into the darkness. I stumbled, and I heard Elizabeth's weeping behind me.

As I felt the wet cold of that passing water, I thought of four women I passed long ago upon a different road. They were washing newly shorn wool against the stones of another stream, laughing, happy over something. Women wiser than I.

The leader thrust me to the rocky ground, then turned me over and pulled apart my wraps.

"Be quick with me," I pleaded.

He struck me hard. His heavy smell overcame me as he

opened my legs. I grasped for the ground, cutting my hand deep on his sword. Then the other pains rolled through me as his weight crushed into my softness. I squeezed my eyes shut.

In time, two more of the thieves would cross through the dark trees to take their turns with me.

~ Twenty-One ~

The thieves disappeared into the night, taking all that they had stolen, along with two sheep and a goat.

The littlest children eventually slept. By dawn all of us were up and moving silently about our rekindled fire, repacking our torn stores and bundles.

The older children rounded up our animals as others fed the fire. The three sisters wept over their dead potter, carrying him off to the tumbling of the cold stream where they disrobed him and bathed him. Then they prayed over him.

My cut hand burned, so I worked one handed at a soup as I watched the sisters strap the potter's upper torso together, unable to see him hurting even in death.

Taking down our own shelter, I silently wove my way through the woes of my own life: the thieves of the night before, then Amon so long ago. I thought of my lost child, and of course, I wondered over the growing, shadowy tale of Him—my mother's brother, the mere mention of whom still caused such trouble, as evidenced mere hours before.

Elizabeth, with little Samuel by her side, packed our burros. I selfishly wished she was thinking of me, but she merely mentioned the bitter cold of that morning, her vapory breath mixed with Samuel's as they worked.

Then she came over to me, close, and whispered, "Mother, I just remembered. In a marketplace in Bethany, back when I was swelling with Samuel, I overheard one woman telling another of this bleeding woman, a woman weakened and saddened and unwanted after having passed her monthly blood without end for twelve years."

"Elizabeth, must you?" I ached. My hand ached as I felt fresh pain between my legs.

"But Mother, this bleeding woman saw your mother's brother moving through a crowd. She had heard of Him, so she made her way through the people. Near to Him, and determined with faith, this woman reached and touched only the hem of His cloak. And her bleeding ceased that very day, that very moment, and she became happy, and—"

"Elizabeth, we have to finish our packing and making the soup," I stopped her, a bleeding woman myself. "Then we must help with the burial of the potter."

~ Twenty-Two ~

The morning stayed cold as the weavers broke away at the rocky ground, digging the potter's grave. Nearby, his washed body was oiled and lovingly wrapped by the three sisters, ready for burial.

Over the shallow hole, the three sisters wept anew. We all said our prayers, learning that his name was David, and as we mourned and prayed, Elizabeth's thoughts again roamed to my mother's brother—for she later told me so, wondering by the graveside why the growing memory of Him seemed so terrible to so many.

I myself, listening to the sacred words, wondered likewise if truth could indeed be something other than the laws of our scribes. Then, as I gazed upon the horizon, memories of the night before seized me. I fought hard then to think of nothingness instead, focusing on the words of our prayers.

Afterward, we all returned to our packing and our animals, pausing only to eat. I spooned the soup with old bread and assorted nuts. The youngest sister ate little and quickly before supporting her widowed sister as she insisted upon returning to David's rocky mound to complete her mourning. I wondered offhandedly if they too had heard of His words regarding pride and folly, avarice and envy, the uncleanliness of the human heart mattering much more than the insisted traditions of our scribes.

Then the men called us to rise. The two sisters had to pull the other, David's wailing widow, from the mound of his rocky grave.

As we moved on from those thin trees, and when I knew that Elizabeth could not see me, I looked back across that cold stream, to where the thieves had taken me.

The grassy spot was lit with gray daylight, and there was a rotting log nearby which I had not seen in the night.

I felt old, leading our willful burro, and my cut hand hurt and quietly I started to cry.

*

Later that morning I was summoned forward by the weavers for water.

The elder brother was telling his father of a Roman highway he believed to be nearby. I poured them water as they discussed the laid roads of fitted rock that the Romans had fashioned for military movements and caravans. The weavers figured the risk of Roman interference well worth the benefit of this modernization that would make our own traveling easier.

By midmorning, a rare light snow fell upon us as our movement paused yet again at the sight of the bloody remains of one of the weaver's stolen animals.

Laying near cinders, and still warm to the touch, the goat's carcass was cut cleanly in half, just as the gazelle's had been.

Night of Romans

~ Twenty-Three ~

After coming upon the goat's carcass, we fearfully kept watch on the horizons while working our way down into softer, drier lands.

The morning stayed cool as the weavers, prompted perhaps by aged Aminah and bug-eyed Turka from the night before, spoke of slavery.

"I've heard it's upwards of one hundred thousand slaves in Rome alone," the younger brother shared.

"And growing by the year, creating a citizenry foreign to man and woman's proper labors," the old man supposed.

Behind us, their distraught wives discussed other matters. I heard them speak first of the youngest sister, then Elizabeth— "the limping one" they called her. The thieves were evil, they assented as we moved amongst our carts and animals, but an evilness acted upon both the innocent and the deserving. And as evil beckons evil, they agreed the Superstitious sister should have been expelled once discovered. Alongside them, their little girl trudged, her head wrapped, her wound still seeping fresh blood.

Behind us, the three sisters wept. One of the children

determinedly led their burdened burro while the other three appeared simply numb.

Amongst the sheep, Elizabeth hobbled strong, Samuel beside her. She caught me and told me, "I'll forever cherish your kindness of last night. I'll never be able to return it."

"I'd never allow it, returning such a misfortune," I answered her. "You know that, for you have a child now too."

She nodded, then went on to share her pondering that morning, of our people's anticipation of our Savior to free us from Rome. Although I did not wish to speak of it, she asked anyway, "Do you ever wonder of His disappointing those who followed Him about?"

"I try not to. I try to *leave Him be*," I told her, sharply but truthfully. She could not understand, nor could I, His *kingdom-not-of-this-world*.

Later, behind thin cedars, I checked myself for more of my bleeding. I thought then of Elizabeth, of her conception, and I felt shame, for I was unable to recall her father's name.

Yet I could recall the wedding ceremony of the family I served back then. I could recall the night air, the feasting, and the cool grasses beneath myself and that man. I could remember the song and the wine and how, like my Jared, Elizabeth's father had stuttered—his only endearment to me that night so long ago.

I've led a life I am not proud of, with three children from three men. And so I tried to pray as we moved onward.

Then our movement halted as our sheep spread out,

bleating. Elizabeth stopped abruptly, little Samuel behind her. A burro brayed. The men were looking to the high ground to our right, so I looked there too.

"Mother!" gasped Elizabeth. "Do you see them?"

"Yes, I do."

Two Romans on horseback, outlined clearly against the moving gray of the sky.

They were helmeted and armored, bearing shields and javelins as they held tight to the reins of their large beasts.

They spoke to one another atop those high rocks, then turned their horses and disappeared.

The weavers talked briefly, making our decision; we pressed on, east for Jericho, beneath the gray sky.

*

In time, the heavy clouds gave way to a steady breeze, but we found no streams. Slowing from thirst, our animals required more and more prodding. The two Romans occupied much of our talk, for there had to be more of them, unless the two we saw were mere couriers of the Empire's messages.

"Not likely," dismissed the elder weaver. "Couriers move alone, hard and constant."

His brother and father agreed. Besides, the two horsemen had appeared watchful and thoughtful from their rocky vantage point.

The men pondered these things before us as the three sisters quieted their grief behind us.

Beside me, Elizabeth and little Samuel steadied our burros as we moved. I heard her tell him, "The day is brightening, Samuel—bound to bring favor to our journeying. Look there!" she added as she pointed toward distant piercings of sunlight, slicing the gray sky before us, kissing the valley beyond.

~ Twenty-Four ~

Burdened with the hard truths of the night before, as well as my renewed deep, womanly pain, I ruminated upon the truths of myself, and those of my mother's brother. I wondered of His wrongs and my own wrongs, my crimes and His. I wondered at how seemingly small wrongs—His, mine, anyone's—could shape themselves, building and spreading, until entire lives had gone astray. And I wondered whether His life or mine had done more harm to the innocent.

Then I was called forward in service to the weavers where I overheard the old man informing his sons, "They were scouts, part of a flank guard of a Roman century, perhaps attached to a full legion somewhere near."

"Foot soldiers, several thousand strong," his one son added. "Maybe they're headed for the copper and iron ore mines south of the Dead Sea where they say rebellious trouble is brewing."

He'd only just finished speaking when his father halted our company for there was a heavy movement upon the eastern horizon.

Through the cool distance we could see a dark line of

Roman legionaries crossing the gray-brown of the land. Dust rose and floated behind them, giving shape to the distant breeze. In the stillness we could hear the faint rumble of their movement across no trail.

They were moving hard—moving toward us.

*

We waited, and shortly we could count their numbers. They were small, only thirty or so strong, but still intimidating as they moved in their rumbling chariots and heavy carts, seven or eight in length.

We soon could see their beardless faces through the slicing sunlight. Then we saw one cart, toward the front of their movement, carrying bound people. Six of them, shackled together, bouncing through the rising dust of the horse soldiers before them.

The prisoners' features resolved into the four thieves and their two slaves, Aminah's wild hair flying in the wind.

*

The Romans strode forward in two columns. The weavers eagerly discussed them, guessing them to be a portion of a cohort, horse soldiers, with five or six more of its size nearby, perhaps part of a full legion of infantry within a day's traveling.

The women wept, gathering the children close.

Saying nothing myself, I observed how the Romans always looked larger than us. Even their horses seemed bigger and heavier as they slowed, angling across the terrain.

As they closed in on us, we could make out their shields, axes, bows, and javelins. The mule train behind them was seven deep, manned by slaves lashing their yoked beasts. The carts also carried two light catapults and were followed by four trains, packed tight, presumably with food, shelter, and more weaponry.

Shortly, the Romans were upon us, their centurion emerging from their dust.

"Who speaks for you people?" His voice was loud and certain. He was helmeted, and his breastplate gleamed, even with the sun obscured. His great horse was lathered with sweat.

"I do!" declared the elder brother. "Allow me to introduce myself."

"Good, good! And a good Saturnalia to you, man!" the centurion answered. "Have your people been wronged recently by thieves?"

"Wronged in which way, dominus?" asked the elder brother. "By highway men, such as those bound in your train, or by common raiders who brought ruin and death to our sacred Jerusalem?"

His younger brother stiffened at his boldness while their aged father postured proud.

"Do not debate me, man, and do not answer my questions with questions," the centurion spat. "I am not of good humor, nor do I care for your politics."

"It was we who were wronged!" the widowed sister cried. "My family by those you have in chains!"

The centurion looked to her, then issued commands in their Latin. His men dismounted behind him, but he remained mounted, moving his great horse up to the weavers.

"We shall sort this business out according to Roman law," the centurion commanded. "You can be of assistance or of interference, though I strongly encourage the former. It is late in our day, and we are ahead of our expected position. We shall make camp here, and so shall you."

"Not us," the elder brother started. "We will not answer to your—"

He was struck hard and fast by the short whip of the centurion, still upon his great horse; I wasn't even aware that he held one. The elder brother stumbled, baffled and hurt. Their elderly father remained silent, his proud posture wilted.

"You and your people will answer to me!" the centurion continued. "And be reminded, I do not take directives from citizens. Something will be done about these six we've come upon. They have been arrested under general suspicion. Separated, they tell two tales."

The centurion glanced across the horizon then back to the eldest brother. "Now, man, are your women and children properly fed?" He looked us over while his sweating horse pawed at the ground. Evidently finding us wanting, he continued, "Well, it is the season of Saturnalia. Rome's dignity will be brought to this wilderness tonight."

*

Elizabeth watched with fearful eyes as the centurion's legionaries moved in concert, fearless of the bound thieves, setting heavy poles to strong rope and raising their large tents. Their horses fed well, tied to anchors driven deep into the rocky ground.

Their fire was built fast—someone's assignment. Other legionaries, dispatched for wood, dragged back whole sections of trees tied to strong, sweating horses. They split and chopped this timber into thick sections while others dug sentry pits around our encampment.

The four thieves and their two slaves were bound, two apiece, to three thick posts, staked uncomfortably close to the fire, awaiting the trial the centurion promised. The two younger thieves were bound together, as were the older thieves. The third post held fast their slaves. Somehow, Aminah slept.

"Perhaps bound according to their separate tales..." I overheard the weavers' father suggest.

I dared to look closer, wishing vengeful thoughts upon the bloodied face of their leader, the one who had dragged me across the cold stream the night before. I later overheard that he'd lost several of his teeth and had his jaw broken from talking back to the centurion. I also learned that the centurion's interest in our party arose from the thieves' desperate accusations of Followers amongst us—accusations the weavers would repeat.

Dust settled about us as we retired to our small shelters. Suckling my infant, I pondered our delicate situation amongst captured thieves, a far-from-home Roman century, and, of course, a Follower in our own company.

I listened to the century's harsh Latin as Elizabeth and Samuel rested. Foreign talk then laughter, over and over. All must have been well with them.

Exhausted and closing in on sleep, my thoughts drifted again to my mother's mother, my grandmother. Mary, she was called. I wondered of this woman who had followed her firstborn better than I'd been able to follow mine.

A woman who had stood fast by her son as other Romans in another time nailed Him to the timber of a cross.

~ Twenty-Five ~

The centurion's fiery trial began after a modest feeding of the legionaries, with water for the prisoners and bread for us. The Romans promised a true feast would follow as befit their Saturnalia.

Above the great fire, stars peeked out, bright and scattered. The centurion's two lieutenants looked up at them, discussing two wanderers and pondering their meaning.

Then the centurion took his central position, standing before a strong chair, perhaps brought along for occasions such as this. His placement was commanding, illuminated by the blaze. He stood tall, his scribe beside him ready to document this wilderness justice.

The centurion began by proclaiming, "I am Centurion Titus Antonius Scipio! I and my lieutenants are of the empire's Antonius gen, a long line of fit centurions and warriors. I alone am commissioned this night, and indeed, I alone will see to the dispatching of sound justice by this fire!"

I would learn later from a meddling Elizabeth that the centurion's lieutenants, Quintus and Manius, were his younger half-brothers. All three shared the same father, but Quintus and Manius were born of their father's much younger second wife, a woman living in far-off Rome, waiting in her centurion's fine domus. Elizabeth learned these things, among other insights, from the youngest brother Manius, who enjoyed talking around the fire.

*

The centurion's first order of justice concerned the slaves, Aminah and Turka- the big-eyed boy. As general housekeeping, they were discussed first, for the centurion's trial would be shaped into two parts: the trial of the thieves, and the accused Followers of the Great Superstition.

Both slaves proclaimed to belong to the two older thieves. They also claimed relation to one another, hailing from people of the deserts east of the River Nile, though neither expected to see their homelands again.

Continuing the trial, the first order of justice was easy. The captured thieves were liars "by virtue of their livelihoods," as stated by the centurion. It remained only a question as to which among them bore the most responsibility for their actions and the most trouble for their lies. "For the truth is the easiest thing to recall," Scipio dictated to his scribe, "and my duty this night is made easier by their own turning upon one another!" Evidently, upon being searched and interrogated earlier, the older thieves had turned on the two younger ones. The opinions of the slaves were never weighed; their testimony only clarified whose responsibility they were.

Upon the centurion's probing, the two older thieves

revealed themselves as Matthan of Zerah and Joram of no man.

Matthan, their leader with the swollen and bloodied face, claimed Palmyra as his homeland, and Joram, Dura Europos as his, explaining their Syrian speech. Both tried to straighten themselves as they took turns answering the centurion, attempting to weave their tales together; they insisted that the younger thieves had been the ones to rob and abuse our caravan while they, courageously for aged men, tried to intervene, to spare us the fate we endured. Matthan meekly mumbled these lies through broken teeth, so unlike his bold taunting the night before.

Of course, the younger thieves, called Jotham of Zerubabel and Saul of unknown parentage, denied such assertions. Saul, the only one who hadn't crossed the stream to have his way with me, wept through the duration of their interrogation.

I looked hard at Saul, studying his dirtied, wet face, trying to measure his years as he confessed being lowly and begged for Roman mercy.

"Perhaps a sound whipping," he pleaded, "followed with an indentured servitude to you, Centurion Scipio?"

Jotham, from lands west of Cana, agreed with Saul's testimony initially. His confession fell short, however, evading the mean pleasure he took upon me. His omission did not pass by Elizabeth, and later that night she whispered again of her love for me for rearing her without a father, for taking her in after her husband's death, and, finishing in tears, for taking her raping.

The centurion then called forward the weavers who

told a third tale—the more true one, which rang closer to that of the younger thieves. They pointed to Matthan as David's murderer while the three sisters wailed anew across the great blaze.

The elder brother then interjected, demanding a like justice for the suspected Follower in our caravan.

"One trial at a time," the centurion reprimanded him as his scribe worked away by the fire's light, "and I remind you, man, I shall tend to these questions, not you."

Then, startling me, the centurion called out, "You, woman taken of the flesh. Come before me!"

I rose. My infant cried, restless at my bosom. Elizabeth tried to take him, but I clung to him as I stepped forth.

"Your name, woman?"

"Rebecca," I answered. "Rebecca of shepherds north of Capernaum."

The centurion looked hard at me. He tilted his head, frightening me.

"Do I know you, Rebecca of shepherds?" he asked me.

"No, dominus, I do not believe so."

"You look familiar to me—you *feel* familiar to me. You nearly haunt me, woman." He smiled, which eased me a bit, then shook his head and resumed his questioning.

"What child is this?" he asked of my infant.

"Mine, dominus."

The women of the weavers murmured, for that was not my story five days before.

"Where is the baby's father?"

"I do not know. I have not always lived by the laws of

my people, Centurion. I have been less than perfect in my conduct."

He paused, then said, "I see. I appreciate your honesty."

"My infant is fatherless," I added, "as is my grown daughter, and her own child. We are traveling alone, away from Jerusalem, welcomed in servitude by these two families."

"I appreciate your circumstances, woman. I need no more knowledge of them." He straightened himself, returning to the business at hand. "Now, the night before this one, were you taken in rape or did you give yourself or sell yourself to these men bound before us?"

I felt the heat of the fire behind me. "I gave myself, dominus, after their apparent interest in my daughter."

"You simply gave yourself without struggle or ulterior design?"

"No, dominus. I had motive. I lied to them regarding my daughter's cleanliness."

"Then you gave yourself? I must repeat this, woman."

"Yes, dominus. I gave myself." Then I braved up and added, "Sometimes it is better to give to thieves what they desire rather than resisting their intentions and losing it all the same."

"Yes, Rebecca of shepherds, I understand."

He examined me, his face lit by that fire. Softly he commanded, "Turn about for me, woman, two times."

I did as he said, turning twice upon the stony ground.

"You do indeed haunt me, woman. Perhaps I once dreamed of one like you—a dream I have forgotten, or one never correctly recalled upon awakening. A silliness, I am certain."

He dismissed me, calling his scribe to readiness.

Speaking loudly and clearly, the centurion first proclaimed immediate freedom for the two slaves, Aminah and Turka, "...as befits the spirit of our Great Saturnalia. My scribe will prepare the proper documents. Of course, either may also choose to remain with this century in servitude, if they so wish."

The boy and the woman whispered fast to one another, then to the scribe, seeming afraid of the centurion. The scribe wrote quickly before excusing them. The two disappeared into the starry Judean night, though their separation was short-lived. By dawn they'd return in servitude —another wilderness decision made.

Lit by the flames, the centurion continued his judgement. "I decree, by the goodwill of the Saturnalia—for both should justly die—Jotham of Zerubbabel and Saul of no one known shall be only flogged, then peacefully set free at dawn. Matthan of Zerah and Joram of no one known shall be crucified at the breaking of camp. This is Rome's justice for these thieves!"

He took a breath, then sat in his big chair.

"Now, I shall hear the accusations against the alleged heretics amongst you."

~ Twenty-Six ~

More timber was ordered. The great fire flared and sparked under its new weight.

The weavers were quick with their accusations, and the soldiers shortly pulled both the pocked-faced sister and Elizabeth before the centurion, who then called over the elder of his two officers.

"Lieutenant Quintus Antonius," he explained, "knows much more about the spreading of this Great Superstition than I myself care to learn."

Their backs lit by the flashing of the great fire, Elizabeth and the sister stood quietly before the centurion, his lieutenant, and his scribe. Beside them, the thieves remained silent as well, still bound to their posts.

"Our own religion is largely the concern of, or perhaps an affair of, our great Roman state," the centurion continued. "Our priests go about their business, as do our soldiers, our engineers, our merchants, our farmers, our fishermen, and our slaves. This business before me now," his voice grew harder, "concerns *your* religion and is yet another matter of Jews turning on Jews. Am I correct, my brother?"

"You are," Lieutenant Quintus answered simply. He was a man of few words, even during the great feasting later that evening, this brother remained the quieter one.

"So, this agitator, this carpenter they worship, lived during Tiberius' reign. Am I correct?"

"You are again, my brother."

"And you two women before me," he redirected, "you embrace this faith? You are of this thinking?"

"Yes," replied the pocked-faced sister without hesitation.

"Why?" the centurion asked.

"Because of the things I have heard," she answered, "and because of the things that I feel. Is not one thousand years long enough for my people to wait?"

"I will ask the questions, young woman," the centurion reminded, gentler and softer than he had with the weavers.

He turned then to Elizabeth. "And you, young woman, do you too hold to this idea?"

"I think I may, dominus, though I am not certain."

"Unsure, are you, of this repugnant belief? Unsure that a criminal's corpse rose from its own grave to prove himself a king of kings—a god amongst you Jews?"

"I am not certain," Elizabeth repeated, glancing briefly at Samuel and me as we watched through the flashing reaches of the flames.

"Our empire covers much of the world," said the centurion, "and we are a learned people with a diverse understanding of beliefs. Cults with their new rituals and promised hopes spring up often, only to wither and die just as quickly. My brother," he called over his shoulder, "what is the protocol for matters such as this one before me?"

The lieutenant responded as though reading the words of another instead of speaking himself, "This particular madness sprouted from the death of a carpenter's son nearly forty years ago—a man in his thirties, hailed from either Nazareth or Capernaum."

"I know this much. Continue, my brother."

"It has affected peoples from as far off as the cold lands of Gaul to the warmer lands of the lower River Nile. It has spread thinly but far. If I may, my brother, I suggest we use the precedence established by the Honorable Pliny in his letters to Trajan. It would be most fitting."

"Go on," Scipio commanded. The fire rippled across the faces of the Romans.

"I am not certain if allowances ought to be made regarding the ages of those found to be suspect, whether they be children or adults, nor whether repentance justifies pardoning, but I do know his method of inspection and its subsequent justice, which is as follows."

The lieutenant paused to take a deep breath, then continued, "The suspected are to be interrogated regarding the nature of their superstition, then asked if they refuse the gods of the Empire in favor of this new cult. Should they confess this to be so, then inspection is to be repeated twice more under the threat of capital punishment, if they persevere. If they persevere all three times, they are to be executed. That, my brother, is Rome's justice."

The centurion's breastplate reflected the flames of the

fire as he turned again to Elizabeth and the youngest sister. "You have heard our established justice. What are your faiths?"

The youngest of the sisters spoke first, so fast as to startle me, "He is my God, the carpenter's son. I am neither sorry nor repentant of this truth."

"And was He a king, young woman?"

"Yes, He is, Centurion."

"Then where is His kingdom, and what goals have His armies achieved? I assure you, young woman, I am not making light of you nor your faith."

"His kingdom is here and everywhere, in the past and this very night and in the future too. He is in my breast and in my mind and in yours too, Centurion, should you care to listen." Then she hung her pock-marked face. "I know nothing of any armies—His, yours, or otherwise."

"You may be silent now," the centurion commanded, then directed his attention to Elizabeth. "And you? Are you of this same heart?"

I wondered of Elizabeth's faith in me and of the night before. I closed my eyes, wishing fervently for her to deny my mother's brother.

"No, dominus," Elizabeth replied slowly. "I am not as certain."

"How so? I do not like uncertainty, young woman."

"I believe- or rather, I wonder- if He, the carpenter's son, was not so much a messenger as a discoverer- a discoverer of a deeper, more beautiful truth. A revealer of a God more true—that He revealed something about God, which includes us all, rich and poor, Roman and Jewish, slave and—"

"Enough! A trial cannot be decided on uncertainty, young woman," the centurion growled. "Your own people's supreme council, your Sanhedrin, found this man-god guilty of blasphemy and now demand the same justice for any Followers of this Superstition."

"A faithful body of righteous men that still exists!" cried the younger weaver from the shadows. "Despite the destruction of our beloved Jerusalem!"

A legionary knocked him to the ground and thrashed him fast with a short whip.

The centurion looked dispassionately at the discipline. "We shall discuss one thing at a time," he ordered softly, a reminder to all about the great blaze. "Such is the order of our empire."

"No," Elizabeth whispered, drawing back the centurion's attention. "I do not believe the growing tales of the carpenter's son. I am of Abraham, and our people of Moses. I faithfully await the coming of our Mashiach to deliver us from Rome. One thousand years is not enough."

The centurion relaxed. "Although not a criticism of my appetite, I must ask you to repeat that sentiment twice more, so that I may return my attention to the woman beside you and be finished with this business."

Elizabeth spoke those words two times more, and he excused her before surprising his lieutenants, declaring, "I now demand an orderly discussion wherein we might sway this young woman away from harsh punishment. It is, after all, Saturnalia, and she has harmed no one." His face, lit by the fire, seemed sad somehow. "Her crime thus far has been only against herself. What else do you know, my brother?"

The quiet lieutenant did not hesitate in his response: "What little else I know comes from my previous posting, patrolling the lands of Patara and Myra. The Followers there, in Lystra and Antioch, have taken to calling this carpenter's son '*Christos*,' the Greek translation for the Hebrew *Mashiach*. Some have shortened this title to '*Christ*'—a new term, my brother."

Murmurings arose from the weavers. The elder brother stepped forth.

"Then they are heretics," he said, "and most blasphemous, if we may speak."

"You may," answered the centurion, "but be mindful of your rank in this discussion."

"Do not take their faith so hard nor so personal," added the quiet lieutenant, smiling. "You Jews have good company in your disdain for this cult. These Followers tax our Roman resources, disobey our Roman laws, and deny our gods in honor of this 'Christos' of theirs, whose own birth, teachings, and deeds remain questionable."

"Share more, my brother. You remain informative," ordered the centurion.

His lieutenant finished, "We have examined these Followers by trial, we have punished them, and we shall continue to do so. Their madness, which poisons simpler minds, shall pass, as have previous others."

A clamor arose from the weavers and their women.

"Silence!" barked the centurion. "If you care to bear

witness to this process, then I shall grant one statement from each of you and no more. I advise you make your testimonies worth contributing—something wise and concise," he added, then grumbled to himself, "the Saturnalia has stretched my charity too far concerning quarrelsome Jews."

So, the weavers each took their turn. I added nothing, for I had heard it all before, but I listened carefully as they shared the tales and whisperings that the foolish and the poor believed. They shared the rumors of His healing of the infirm, of His quieting storms, and one even told of His impossible feeding of many from meager stores of loaves and fish. All expressed earnest concern over His missing body following His crucifixion, which had led His most rabid followers to claim He'd risen from the dead.

They spoke of the men and women who followed Him as He wandered. I listened on, fearing their anger if they knew my relation, afraid even the mention of my family could somehow be traced back to me, but they were more focused on His followers and what such company suggested of Him. One tale reported a loving whore at the foot of His cross.

"...which should only discount this madness all the more!" the aged weaver proclaimed.

"Enough," the centurion decided, holding up his hand. "This queer fable of yours should not be Rome's problem." Then he took a deep breath. "However, on this night the growing memory of this man has decidedly become my own."

Centurion Scipio called his scribe to attention. Then he

turned to the pocked-faced sister who stood alone before the great fire.

"What is it, exactly, that your man-god wanted or wished for in His time? Again, I do not mock you."

The youngest of the sisters stood with her dark hair falling about the sides of her face, as it had the previous night amongst the thieves. She raised her eyes boldly. "I cannot answer many of your questions. Whether He is dead now or gone off elsewhere, I do not know. But I believe that He is our Savior at last. Nothing less."

"Young woman," the centurion said quietly, "I must ask you the same as I asked of the lame woman. Two more times, and if you persevere, I must condemn you to death alongside these thieves."

Her face fell before the centurion. Shrouded by the light of the fire, she proclaimed softly, "He is my God, Centurion, my 'Christos' from Nazareth, by way of Capernaum. And He is with me now, this night, even before this fire."

Without waiting to be asked, she repeated her words twice more.

Across the great blaze, her sisters and their children wept anew, as not a day had passed since the killing of their David.

~ Twenty-Seven ~

The youngest sister was bound to the posting that earlier had held the slaves, Aminah and the big-eyed boy. A single legionary, equipped with a battle ax, guarded all three postings.

Lit torches, pitched about the encampment cast yellow light and carried a thick smell of oil. The Romans feasted and drank heartily, as was their right on Saturnalia. The lieutenants offered reasonable stores to whomever cared to join them. They also appropriated three of our sheep and six of our chickens to kill and cook for their celebrating.

It was the youngest brother, Lieutenant Manius, who approached our shelter with his Roman cheer. Reflections of the fire rippled forth on his light armor. His Hebrew was simple.

"I wish I had jellyfish and eggs—my favorites," he smiled. "However, we must make do with sow's udders stuffed with salted sea urchin. This boy will like it, I am certain," he said, waving his food beneath Samuel's nose.

Elizabeth and I were courteous, hoping for food. Two legionaries, apparently his friends, joined him at our shelter's opening. Together, they reminisced of their own homes: distant Rome for the lieutenant and the shores of the Black Sea for the other two. Manius talked the most, telling tales his friends had clearly heard before, yet we all listened closely as he recollected the plays he'd attended as a boy. He adored comedies where slaves made fools of their masters—stories adored, he claimed, for their absurd situations and outcomes. Then he spoke of his favorite players and of the masks they wore, enchanting his friends and us as we ate.

Elizabeth braved up, asking him of Rome's great tenement buildings that stacked people high above their needed fire and water, of the grand monuments, of city streets so busy that cart and wagon traffic was only permitted at night.

Through his full mouth, Lieutenant Manius happily confirmed these stories before shifting to his boyhood education. His friends, feasting heartily beside him, nodded along with his tales of his enslaved Greek instructors.

"Enslaved they are, such is Rome's respect for the Greek mind," Lieutenant Manius reminded us, which led him to his boyhood parchments of history, astronomy, geometry, "...and the severe thrashings delivered to any inattentive boy." Here he smiled, though his mouth remained full of food.

"Do your girls learn to read and write too?" Elizabeth asked.

"They may at home," the Lieutenant answered, "should their mothers care to teach them and if anyone cared to teach their mothers!" He and his friends laughed heartily at that. "But usually," he returned to Elizabeth, who shied up, "our girls learn music and the knowledge of seeing to a household and its servants, as with your people."

In his faulty Hebrew, Manius talked of his family's fine history of soldiering. He swelled with pride over his brother having become a centurion, just as their grandfather and his father before him. He waxed lyrical on the beauty of their Saturnalia, the ending of yet another fine Roman year. Then he spoke of their gods, chuckling over Saturn's son, Jupiter, with his many mistresses and liaisons with goddesses and mortals alike, siring multitudes of children in spite of his stormy marriage.

"What a god of gods should be!" the young lieutenant proclaimed proudly.

Then one of the legionaries asked him his opinion of this business of the Great Superstition.

"A foolish cult," Manius assured him. "A dangerous one at that, urging the desperate away from long-settled laws. It is unruly, and therefore, it is not good."

He glanced at Elizabeth. She may have denied the faith, but her tentative contemplation, though momentary, would not soon be forgotten.

"I once heard," said the other soldier, "of a woman washing this man's feet then drying them with her own hair, as though He was truly a king!"

My infant roused, and I busied myself nursing him by torchlight, frightened by this turn in conversation.

Then Elizabeth spoke her mind, dangerously so, "Perhaps His kingdom is not a place. Perhaps it is a devotion, not unlike that girl's. A kingdom within, a separate and common caring. A godliness within each of us, should we so choose. We can allow Him into our hearts, you see, and—"

Loud horns sounded abruptly, startling me and piercing that starry night.

Young Lieutenant Manius studied Elizabeth's face by the torchlight. "Be cautious, young woman, with your thoughts and your words," he said. "Too many people are too much divided."

Then he stood and smiled. "I bid your family good night."

Their trumpeters sounded again, this time long and mournfully, summoning the centurion's soldiers to sleep.

In the Kingdom of
the Wind

~ Twenty-Eight ~

The trumpeters' horns pierced the cold dawn of the morning.

The Romans rose to duty. Embers of their fire were stoked. Legionaries and heavy horses startled our animals that had stilled for the night.

Within our shelter, I watched as their large tents came down in collapsing folds to hand signals and hearty Latin shouts.

The sentries returned from their postings, Aminah and the big-eyed boy with them, as kettles stewed a rich steam over the new licking of their great flame.

Elizabeth spotted the proud centurion moving through the early morning smoke with his lieutenants in tow, inspecting his soldiers' work.

"Are you okay?" she asked me as she examined my cut hand, noting my glance toward the four thieves and the youngest sister. All remained bound, slumped in despair. Two awaited severe whippings; three, their own deaths. I shook my head, thoughts too complicated to speak.

A fast breakfast followed. The Romans were again

kind, sharing their food with us. The prisoners were given nothing.

Another trumpeting prompted a quick packing of the century's chariots and carts. Another brought order before the centurion himself.

The men assembled in rank, aligning near the bound prisoners. The fire's smoke swirled up into the bluing sky. Its heat warped the Romans standing to order before their commander.

Scipio spoke loudly, "The executions shall commence. I am informed that our infantry to the west has caught up to us. We shall march hard, regaining our forward flanking!" Then, without ceremony he continued, "The remaining timber will suffice for the crucifixions."

The older thief wept through the bloody and broken mess of his lower face as the two younger thieves were unbound and stripped.

"You are forgiven. Be grateful to the spirit of the Great Saturnalia!" the centurion proclaimed. "Now, on your knees!"

The criminals, naked and dirty, obeyed. Two legionaries worked quickly and severely, scourging the thieves' fleshy backs for their promised scars.

Satisfied, the centurion inquired, "Have you any words before you are cast free?"

"Thank you, and blessed be the Empire," mumbled the one who had enjoyed his own crime against me. He trembled, splattered with his own blood.

"Thrash me more," the quieter one choked out, "if it might spare the girl, she who follows the Great

Superstition." He too glistened with the red of his own blood. "My crime is greater than hers. Her only crime is love, Centurion, only love. I beg you to allow my wretched nakedness to come to something better."

"Your sentences have been cast, Saul the thief," Scipio answered. "Be pleased, for Rome has been kind. Both of you, arise!"

The two younger thieves stumbled to their feet, bloody and naked.

"Does anyone have words for these two before they are cast into the wilderness?" the centurion asked.

All remained quiet. Then the youngest sister, still bound to her post, spoke, "What do you know of Him, thief—the carpenter's son, the One I shall die for?"

"Answer her," the centurion demanded, "for she is doomed."

Saul took his time answering. "I have been to Capernaum. I have heard tales and whisperings, but that is all. Still, I ask for another sound thrashing in return for your pardon."

"You know nothing more?" the bound sister asked through her dark hair. Her sisters wept anew behind her.

"No more. Only that those who followed Him about are now old and dying, and that proper Jews shall find truth and peace only through the laws of our Torah and—"

"And are we not Jews?" the bound sister cried into his words. "We still seek His temple, His law! But we have come to adore the carpenter's son, finding God not in our temples, but within us, as He has asked of us."

Then she cried out tearfully, "God's work amongst us

is our very own! We must allow Him into our hearts. His work becomes ours once we love Him as He loves us."

"Silence!" the centurion commanded. "I asked for words, not debate. Now, would anyone else wish to speak? The sun has nearly risen."

Then I myself stepped forth, toward the young thief still on his knees.

"Who is your mother, Saul? And who is your father?" I asked softly.

He looked up at me, his eyes sad and lost. "Criminals have no parents. We left them, and we can never go back."

"Could you be the son of the money changer, the trader Amon of Jeremiah, once of Bethsaida then Capernaum?"

"I have no mother or father. Be done with me, good woman."

"I am not a good woman. I seek a lost son that I—"

"Enough!" the centurion roared. "Step back, woman! Wrap yourselves, you two, with Rome's generous rags and be gone!"

At this, both younger thieves wrapped themselves—a struggle in their state—then hobbled off into the west without another word or glance.

The youngest sister and the two older thieves were unbound, forced to their knees, and thrashed quickly by three Romans with short whips while other soldiers erected crosses behind them, propped by heavy rocks.

When all was ready, the centurion summoned his scribe to read out his verdict from the night before. The two older thieves went first, crying and begging as they were stripped naked, beaten again, and tied cruelly tight to their separate boughs.

Then they were raised. No swords or javelins were ordered.

"They will die in good time, by the day's cold or by time itself," Scipio declared.

Next, he silenced all for the killing of the youngest sister.

"Quintus!" he summoned the quieter brother. "I again require your counsel."

To which Elizabeth abruptly stood and limped forward, startling me. "Take me, Centurion! Take me in place of her!"

I lunged after her, trying to pull her down to the rocky ground.

"Be still!" the centurion commanded as a legionary thrashed us both three times, catching my infant with his last.

"This madness—these women—my brother, is there anything more you can tell me?"

The lieutenant answered quietly, "Your words 'madness' and 'women' are fitting. It seems to be a superstition of the poorest Jews and, curiously, more alluring to their women than their men."

A light wind picked up and pulled at the feathers of the centurion's helmet as his scribe scribbled away.

The lieutenant continued, "The sightings, the hearsay, the nonsense, nearly all of it comes from these sorts. This carpenter's army is swordless, without javelins or shields.

They are bowless and harmless; they are hopeless, my brother."

The older thief cried out from his cross with the lieutenant's last words, evidently reminding the centurion of the task at hand.

"We must be moving on!" Scipio called out. "These shall be my final words for my scribe and for your ears, my legionaries, and for you Jews!" He breathed deep into the breeze of the dawning sky. "Two others have stepped forth, offering themselves in place of this young woman on our beloved Saturnalia's final day. For this, with Rome's mercy entrusted to me and in the spirit of our holiday, I spare her. I pardon her, despite our laws. But I can allow no more charity than this for these Jews!"

He paused again, inhaling once more. "Her back shall be bared and flogged to be scarred. Then she shall go free with my final instruction, which is this: she must swear never to spread this thinking, her illness, amongst others."

He approached the youngest of the sisters still on her knees before him. He waved his scribe away before quietly asking her, "Are you people—that is, those who believe as you do in this carpenter's son—are you Jews or are you something else?"

"I do not know, Centurion," she spoke through her hair. "That is my truth."

"Where are his temples? Where are his shrines, young woman?"

"They are where He built them," she said. "His shrines stand wherever anyone acts from His truth. They stand wherever anyone breaks bread in memory of Him. His temples are within our hearts—a faith, Centurion, as simple as a child's. His temples are built whenever and wherever anyone thinks of Him or whispers to Him, for He listens. That is our prayer, which He has given to us, and to you too."

I was stunned by her words, her repeating of those very words I had heard upon His lap in that grove so long ago. *Of faith and of wishes as pure as a child's.* Of that reminder of His promise that *He listens.*

And I believed.

And oh, how truly I believed that I could talk to Him, that I did right then, without shame!

I thanked Him for my newfound peace, for my own life. I thanked Him for my children and for His presence amongst us. I told Him, in my mind, so earnestly that cold morning, that I loved Him. And I begged Him for His forgiveness.

Then I heard the centurion instruct the youngest sister, "Never teach this madness. Do not spread it. Do you hear me, young woman?"

"Yes, I hear you," this sister replied, her head still down, her hair moving with the breeze.

"You will be set free to return to your family after your requisite whipping. And bless the Great Saturnalia, young woman, for Rome has kissed you."

Her back was stripped naked as she was put to her hands and knees. She, her hair, and her bosom shook and rocked as her back was slashed and bloodied.

Then the trumpeters sounded again, ending her lashing, and the legionaries mounted their waiting horses.

Centurion Scipio turned his own great stead hard about over the rocky terrain to face me and my infant, Elizabeth, and little Samuel.

Our sheep scattered, the wayward burro brayed, and I, unsure why, handed my infant to Elizabeth, for something was swelling within me.

The centurion dismounted and frightened me by approaching us. He grasped my arm and led me strongly some distance across the rocky ground. His sheathed sword slapped against my wrapped thigh, and I remembered Rome's might.

"Woman, you still haunt me," he whispered, turning me about. "Now, stronger than before. Perhaps it is something strange in this wind...I do not know."

I said nothing but kept my eyes fixed on his.

"Listen to me," he spoke quietly, so low I could hear the crackling of their dying fire over his every word. "My mercy for the pocked-faced girl is this—and I do not know why I need to tell you this. It is as though something borne of this wind is upon me, a ghost or something akin to one, like a gentle pest.

Nevertheless, my story is this: I grew up the son of another centurion, my father, a man and a soldier far greater than I. I was raised upon the northern shore of Lake Tiberius—the Sea of Galilee to you Jews."

He paused long enough that I asked, "How may I serve you, Centurion?" For I did not understand the meaning of his tale.

"Hold your tongue, strange woman, and listen carefully," he hushed me, then half-smiled. "This thing, this ghost, this spirit-pest within me has demands."

He continued his tale, "My own mother passed away when I was but a small child, so my father's servant, a Syrian girl, reared me. I loved her dearly. Then one day she fell terribly ill, ill enough my father sought help. And though she recovered, later—" the centurion breathed harder. "—later she, my precious Syrian girl, told me that my father had sought out this carpenter's son, that it was this man-god who had saved her."

His face and speech both tightened, taunt with the memory. "My father never told me this tale, for it is nonsense, but our Syrian girl did, many times. She told it like a secret and sometimes as a lullaby."

"She claimed, Rebecca of shepherds, that this carpenter's son saved her from afar, never stepping foot in our home. He healed her through words alone, citing my father's steadfast faith, as simple and true as a child's, as instrumental in saving an obedient servant for his young son: me."

A small sound escaped me. I inhaled sharply. The wind pushed against us, blowing my hair across my face.

"I do not believe this story," the centurion went on, "but due to it, I have spared these young women—the pocked-faced one and the hobbling one that is your own. And I have words for you too, strange woman." His grasp on me tightened. "Again, I do not know where these words come from. It is as though that ghost, that voice still upon me or within me, now wishes to speak to you."

He half-smiled again. "Oh, woman, you *do* haunt me. This much is true."

Behind him one of the thieves moaned as the dawning sun broke the horizon. The sun had risen.

The century stood patiently across the dying fire. Several of their horses snorted and pawed at the ground.

The centurion whispered, "My words for you, Rebecca of shepherds, are these: An old man thinks of you. He awaits you this very morning. He has sought you, and he has never forgotten you."

His Roman face blurred through my tears.

"He is a shepherd," the centurion added as another wind whipped my hair from my face.

I reached to his chest, touching a seam in his armor, feeling my mother's brother suddenly alive inside me, stronger and more beautiful.

I felt a warmth across my hand. I looked to my palm. *Healed.*

The centurion grasped my healed hand, and he kissed it. I saw a tear in his eye. "His name is Jared," he told me, "And he has found a younger man called Saul, but he has not found you. Both await you, Rebecca of shepherds, upon the eastern shore of your Sea of Galilee."

"Go now, good woman, and seek peace," the Roman added before returning to his century to ride off into the wind.

In the Name Publishing Co.

Milton Keynes UK
Ingram Content Group UK Ltd.
UKHW021014110624
444053UK00014B/696

9 798987 615980